W9-CHG-386
N+C

The HEARTSTOPPER YEARBOOK

Also by

ALICE OSEMAN

HEARTSTOPPER

Volume One

Volume Two

Volume Three

Volume Four

The Heartstopper Coloring Book

Solitaire

Radio Silence

I Was Born for This

Loveless

Nick and Charlie

This Winter

The HEARTSTOPPER YEARBOOK

ALICE OSEMAN

The Heartstopper Yearbook was originally published in the United Kingdom by Hachette Children's Group in 2022.

ISBN 978-1-338-85389-6

10 9 8 7 6 5 4 3 2   22 23 24 25 26

Printed in China 201
This edition first printing, October 2022

CONTENTS

Hello and welcome to the Heartstopper Yearbook!
My name is Alice, and I'm the writer and illustrator of the Heartstopper graphic novel series.

I've wanted to create a Heartstopper art book for many years, but this book has become something so much more. It's a celebration of the entire journey of Heartstopper so far, from the first sketches in 2013 to a Netflix show in 2022, and it's been made possible thanks to the incredible support for the series from readers all around the world.

There's loads I'm excited to share with you in this book, such as my very first sketches of Nick and Charlie, a new comic about Tara and Darcy's origin story, and even a guide to show you how to draw the characters of Heartstopper. And I'll be popping my head in at various points in the book to tell you all about the art, the story, the creation process, and more.

I hope the artwork – old and new – puts a smile on your face!

Alice x

Hey, my name is
Alice
PROFILE PAGE
NAME
Alice Oseman
BIRTHDAY
October 16th
OCCUPATION
Writer/illustrator
PRONOUNS
she/they
LIKES
comics
Digimon
Italian food
DISLIKES
crowds
getting up early
horror
Hello! I'm the creator, writer, and illustrator of Heartstopper! I'm pretty introverted, and a bit of a workaholic, but I love getting to spend every day working on creative projects.

The Tourist - Radiohead
0:00

hello, my name is
Nick
PROFILE PAGE
NAME
Nick Nelson
BIRTHDAY
September 4th
SCHOOL YEAR (IN VOLUME ONE)
Year 11
PRONOUNS
he/him
LIKES
• sports
• Marvel
• dogs
DISLIKES
• bullies
• horror movies
• bugs
When creating Nick, I wanted him to be a gentle giant – a "lad" on the outside, but a sweet and caring boy on the inside. He's often rightly compared to a golden retriever, and he's a go-with-the-flow kind of person.

RUGBY
Treats
for dogs
Everywhere - Fleetwood Mac
0:00

Charlie is the first Heartstopper character who came into existence! I created him for my first YA novel, *Solitaire*. He's an overthinker, introverted, and a little bit of a nerd, but he has a quiet confidence in who he is and what he wants out of life.

10:00
HOMER
The Odyssey
Boyfriend - Best Coast
0:00

PRIDE

Since Heartstopper features a whole bunch of LGBTQ+ characters, I've drawn a lot of Pride-themed Heartstopper art over the years. Pride can mean different things to different people – it can be a protest, a celebration, an identity, a way to find friends and family, and more, or a combination of many of those things. I've always loved drawing the Heartstopper gang finding strength, love, joy, and power in their LGBTQ+ identities!

While LGBTQ+ rights have come a long way in some parts of the world, there's still lots of work to be done. As well as celebrating their LGBTQ+ pride, the Heartstopper gang would take a stand and fight for LGBTQ+ rights, too, such as protesting for healthcare equality for trans people and gender-recognition law reform.
TRANS RIGHTS
PRIDE IS A PROTEST
PROTECT TRANS KIDS
TRANS RIGHTS ARE HUMAN RIGHTS
THE FUTURE ISN'T BINARY
#L WITH THE T

SNAP
SNAP

SNAP
Happy Pride!!

happy pride!

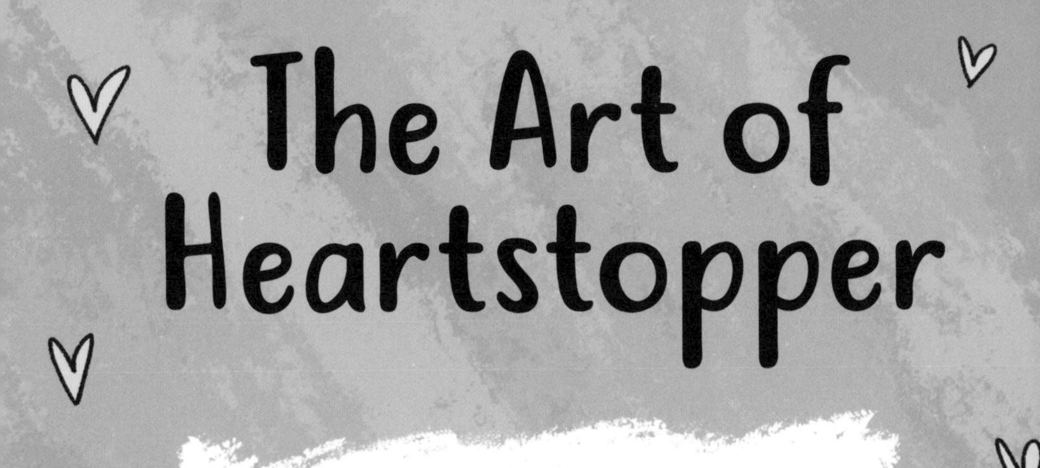

The Art of Heartstopper

Heartstopper has a long and complex history! I began posting the comic online in 2016, but the first time I drew Nick and Charlie was in 2013, when I was in the process of publishing my first novel, *Solitaire*. In the years since then, I've done hundreds upon hundreds of drawings – many of them of the Heartstopper characters – and my art style and Nick's and Charlie's designs have changed a lot.

So let me take you into the past, to when I drew Nick and Charlie for the first time ...

2013

The first drawings I can find of Nick and Charlie were from 2013. I was eighteen, and that was the year I got a publishing deal for my first novel, *Solitaire*, in which Nick and Charlie are secondary characters and are already in a solid, loving relationship. But I loved them as characters and couldn't help but wonder ... how did they get together?

In a couple of cheap sketchbooks, I drew two short comics about Nick and Charlie's origin story – aka how they got together. Story-wise, they're both quite different, and neither of them is particularly accurate to the eventual story of Heartstopper! But even in these very early drawings, you can see the Heartstopper style starting to emerge. I think drawing these two comics is what made me fall in love with Nick and Charlie's story and become determined to tell it properly someday!

I don't have many other sketches of Nick and Charlie from this time. But here's one! I believe this is the first drawing I ever did of Charlie Spring!

STOPS...
WHAT'S YOUR NAME?
CHARLIE
I'M NICK
CHARLIE SPRING.
I COULDN'T BELIEVE
HEY, NICK!
I HADN'T SEEN HIM BEFORE
NICK!!
IS THIS IT?
FORM 13?!
HE'S IN MY NEW FORM?
TUESDAY
HEY
HEY.

2014

I got my first-ever graphics tablet – a Wacom Bamboo – in 2013, but I didn't use it to draw my characters until 2014. These are the first digital drawings I ever did of Nick and Charlie! I was using a piece of free drawing software called GIMP and had mostly no idea what I was doing, but I had a lot of fun figuring out what all the buttons did.

2015

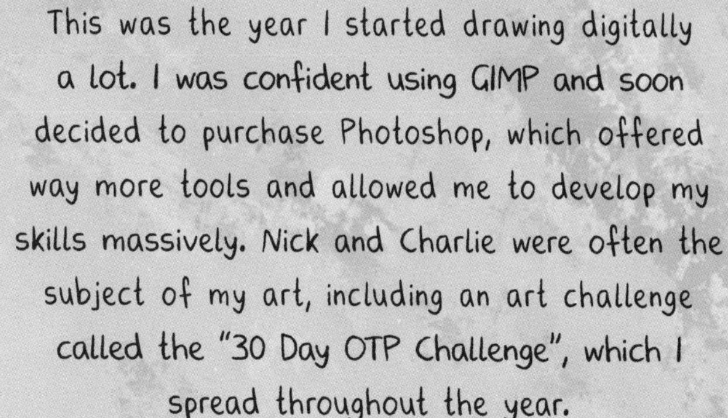

This was the year I started drawing digitally a lot. I was confident using GIMP and soon decided to purchase Photoshop, which offered way more tools and allowed me to develop my skills massively. Nick and Charlie were often the subject of my art, including an art challenge called the "30 Day OTP Challenge", which I spread throughout the year.

normal
clothes

can I kiss you?
yeah

ALICE OSEMAN
RED HEAD
NICK & CHARLIE
NICK..

happy valentine's day<3

2016

I also drew loads in 2016! I experimented a lot with my style and would often just draw very quick doodles rather than a lot of time-consuming full-color illustrations. I did a few more art challenges – an AU challenge, which gave me prompts for different alternate universes and scenarios to draw my characters in, and emoji challenges, where my Tumblr followers would send me emoji suggestions and I'd have to draw my characters with those expressions.

2016 was also the year that I started creating Heartstopper. I was in my final year of university, and around May – most likely after my exams finished – I started drawing Heartstopper pages. I drew around fifty pages before launching the comic on Tumblr and Tapas in September 2016.

Stop making fun of me!
er- you- you had an eyelash on your cheek-

So this is my boyfriend: Charlie!
Pfft!
Their first kiss
...

NICK NELSON
AGE 16
ALICE OSEMAN
what?
haha you were spacing out!

52w
nicholassssssz
204 likes
nicholassssssz it's valentine's day #3 but i thi
pizza more than me
cfspring ur third-wheeling so bad in this
nicholassssssz
2h
397 likes
nicholassssssz in a taxi on the way to a fancy valentine's day
#4 dinner.... apparently we're one of those couples now
cfspring oh god we are aren't we
nicholassssssz @cfspring next thing you know we'll be
paying for a couple's photoshoot
1w
nicholassssssz
230 likes
nicholassssssz ... guess i'll sleep on the floor then
cfspring lol oops
nicholassssssz
2w
th time squad @cfspring

2017

My intense drawing habits slowed down a little in 2017, but I still produced many detailed full-color pieces. I tried out more brushes and coloring techniques, which didn't always work, but every piece helped me to improve. I also drew Tara and Darcy for the first time in color, and I often drew Nick and Charlie aged up, imagining their lives at university or as adults.

Also in 2017, I started to redraw Heartstopper in preparation for a physical edition. My art style had changed a lot since I began the comic in 2016, so to make the artwork more consistent – and to make it something I felt truly proud of – I redrew most of the pages in Chapters 1 and 2. I didn't finish this process until March 2018!

DING
DING
WIN A STUFFED ANIMAL
...
!!

...
AFTER
UM.. r u ok

ALICE OSEMAN
2/14 - All dressed up and ready for Valentine's Day Ball!

ORIGINAL!

RE-DRAWN

ORIGINAL!

RE-DRAWN

Charlie and
a reindeer
Sleepy

sqvishy
pls
snicker
snicker

2/14- The only reason I'm still with this nerd is so he can catch spiders at 3am

RUDE

2018

This was a big year for Heartstopper – I successfully ran a Kickstarter campaign to self-publish the first volume. I felt like Heartstopper's audience was growing massively, along with my own following on social media. I also accepted an offer of publication from Hachette (the publisher who has published all the Heartstopper books in the UK)!

!!
Elle Argent

LEARN
SPANISH
A HISTORY OF WW2

A puppy? For us to keep?
Yes, sweetheart!
Oh, baby, don't cry!!
sniff She's s-so cuuute

It's not THAT many!!

2019

Volumes One and Two of Heartstopper were released by Hachette in 2019 – Heartstopper was officially in bookshops! Alongside this, Heartstopper was in the process of being optioned for TV by See-Saw Films. It was certainly another big year for Heartstopper!

I just realised why I was obsessed with Doctor Who when I was a kid
Charlie. Charlie, wake up.
PAT PAT
mn-what-
...wha
David Tennant.
I always knew I had a crush on Billie Piper because, like, obviously, but I was so obsessed with David Tennant as well, I had all these posters of him on my wall when I was, like, eleven, and I even got my mum to make me a costume so I could go as him for Halloween so I guess I always thought I wanted to be him but actually I also just wanted him, so it-
Nick.
Nick. Please let me sleep.
Nick.

HEARTSTOPPER
VOLUME ONE
IS OUT NOW!

HEARTSTOPPER
VOLUME TWO IS OUT NOW!
...hi
N-Nick

BORK

Thank you!

Pfft-Nick!
happy valentine's day!

2020

I spent all of 2020 writing the scripts for the TV adaptation of Heartstopper, along with writing my fourth YA novel, but I still managed to draw some art pieces I was really happy with. This was the year I started to feel very proud of my art style and how far I'd come as an artist!

HEARTSTOPPER

CHARLIE (AND KITTY)
(They argued)
TORI
SNAP
PARIS
CITY MAP

CHARLIE & NICK
DARCY & TARA
!!
ELLE & TAO

2021

In 2021, I spent three months on the set of the Heartstopper TV show. It was the strangest, most stressful, and most exciting experience of my life, and I still can't quite believe it happened. A lot of my art from this year was inspired by that experience, especially reliving the beginning of the Heartstopper story again, this time in live action.

MUSIC
THE ODYSSEY
Z
Z
Z

MUSIC
THE ODYSSEY
z z z

You're probably the best friend I've... e-ever... had...
I've liked girls before...
but now... I like you
You like me?!
erm... s-so... I just-

Do you wanna sleep?
Hey, I made you some tea
Thanks
It's not beanie weather!
Good luck!
hi!

2022

And now we reach the present – or at least, the present for me! Maybe it's 2122 when you're reading this and the aliens have landed.

I miss the days when I had the time and energy to draw for fun all the time. My life is so busy now that I struggle to create even half as many art pieces in a year as in 2016! But perhaps when Heartstopper is complete, I'll have the time to start experimenting with my art again. Experimenting with art is the best way to develop as an artist, and I look forward to seeing how my art style changes and grows as I get older.

Hello, my name is
Tara
PROFILE PAGE
NAME
Tara Jones
BIRTHDAY
July 3rd
SCHOOL YEAR (IN VOLUME ONE)
Year 11
PRONOUNS
she/her
LIKES
• pastel colors
• anime
• traveling the world
DISLIKES
• watching sports
• public speaking
• storms
Tara is a joy to be around – she's not as loud and talkative as her girlfriend, but she brings light and laughter wherever she goes. Tara's struggled with her sexuality in the past but has since found her inner confidence. She still has a lot to figure out about her future, though.

hydrate
ultra
Silk Chiffon - MUNA, Phoebe Bridgers
0:00

Hey, my name is
Darcy
PROFILE PAGE
NAME
Darcy Olsson
BIRTHDAY
January 9th
SCHOOL YEAR (IN VOLUME ONE)
Year 11
PRONOUNS
she/her
LIKES
• theme parks
• sweets
• storms
DISLIKES
• math
• making decisions
• wearing dresses
Darcy is the chaotic gremlin of the group – the mischievous jokester with bleached hair and scuffed shoes. She doesn't have a great home life, so she always tries to live life to the fullest when she's hanging out with her friends.

gum
gum
yo yo
gum
Tongue Tied - Grouplove
0:00

Hi, my name is Elle
PROFILE PAGE
NAME
Elle Argent
BIRTHDAY
May 4th
SCHOOL YEAR (IN VOLUME ONE)
Year 11
PRONOUNS
she/her
LIKES
• thrifting
• seventies fashion
• iced coffee
DISLIKES
• confrontation
• PE
• camping
Elle is always thinking about her next creative project. She can sometimes shut herself away, busy dreaming up new ideas and creating paintings, drawings, and outfits, but she always loves spending time with the Paris Gang.

sketch book
Elle Argent
Apple Cider - beabadoobee
0:00

Hey, my name is Tao
PROFILE PAGE
NAME
Tao Xu
BIRTHDAY
September 23rd
SCHOOL YEAR (IN VOLUME ONE)
Year 10
PRONOUNS
he/him
LIKES
• Bean (his cat)
• arthouse films
• Polaroid cameras
DISLIKES
• "lads"
• heights
• moths
At the beginning of Heartstopper, Tao tended to interfere in Nick and Charlie's romance, but I love how passionately Tao cares about his friends. I also think Tao doesn't realize how talented, smart, and creative he really is – he's a little lost soul in a beanie!

Me & You Together Song - The 1975
0:00

SUMMER

School's finished for the year, the sun is (hopefully) out, and the Heartstopper gang gets some time to relax and have fun! While we usually get only a few weeks of hot weather in the UK every year, the Heartstopper gang makes the most of it with beach trips, picnics in the park, and vacations with their families.

I love the thought of Nick and Michael tagging along to the Spring family vacation. A week by the pool in Spain or the South of France!

Tori
Michael
SIP
Oliver
Z Z Z

miss you
Miss you too

Mr. Farouk and Mr. Ajayi both enjoy an active summer holiday – they like to see and do stuff, not just sit by a pool! After they get together, they love taking cheap city breaks to see some historical landmarks, art, and architecture.

ARE YOU MORE NICK ... OR MORE CHARLIE?

Question 1: What is your favorite season?

a) Winter – it's full of snow days spent wrapped up in woolly clothes

b) Summer – the perfect season for the beach

Question 2: Which skill would you rather have?

a) Play the drums like a rock star

b) Bake the perfect cheesecake

Question 3: What is your favorite fashion accessory?

a) A snuggly oversized sweater that you've "borrowed" from your partner

b) Patterned socks, especially if they have dogs on them!

Question 4: Which school subject are you better at?

a) Math – Pi is a piece of cake

b) Languages – *tu aimes parler français!*

Question 5: What types of sports do you prefer?

a) Solo sports like running, so you can be alone with your thoughts and listen to music

b) Team sports like rugby that you can play with your friends

Question 6: What posters do you have on your bedroom walls?
a) Your favorite bands
b) Your favorite films

Question 7: Would you describe yourself as an introvert or an extrovert?
a) Introvert
b) Extrovert

Question 8: Would you rather spend your day indoors or outside?
a) Indoors curled up with a good book
b) Outside taking in the fresh air on a walk with your dog

Question 9: You're in Paris! What are you most excited to do in the City of Love?
a) Visit the famous Shakespeare and Company bookshop, of course!
b) Eat all the ice cream!
And practice your French when you order ...

Question 10: Which film would you rather watch?
a) *Moonlight* – it's a modern classic
b) *The Avengers* – all your favorite superheroes in one film? Yes, please!

Question 11: Which personality type best describes you?
a) The Crafter – you enjoy having time to think alone, and you are fiercely independent
b) The Caregiver – you are outgoing and gain energy from interacting with other people

Question 12: What is your biggest weakness?
a) You struggle to open up to others
b) You sometimes feel the need to seek approval from others

Question 13: What is your comfort drink/snack?
a) A cozy cup of tea
b) Buttery toast ... mmm ...

Question 14: It's a new school term and your teacher has sat you next to your crush. What do you do?
a) Smile awkwardly and try to play it cool while secretly hoping that they notice you
b) Say "hi!" and invite them to join your sports team so you have an excuse to be close to them

Question 15: What is your greatest strength?
a) Your passion and imagination
b) Your kindness and loyalty

Question 16: Who is your celebrity crush?
a) Henry Maddox
b) Zooey Deschanel

Question 17: Fountain pen or keyboard?
a) Typing, for sure
b) Fountain pen – maybe not all the time, but you love how it makes your handwriting look

Question 18: And finally, the most important question of all ... are you a cat person or a dog person?
a) A dog person! You can't wait to get your own puppy
b) A cat person ... nah, just kidding, it's dogs every day of the week for you

Mostly As – You're Charlie!
Shy, smart, and a little nerdy, you are just like Charlie! You enjoy your own company and would rather stay home with your books than party all night, but you're also incredibly brave and willing to put the needs of others before your own.

Mostly Bs – You're Nick!
You love any excuse to be outdoors, and you're not afraid to get down and dirty in a game of rugby, but you're also sweet, sensitive, and a loyal friend who is always there in times of need.

The Teachers
a heartstopper mini-comic

This mini-comic is from 2019!

. . . hi.
. . .
Nathan.

Are you even allowed to be here? You don't teach here.

Probably not, but . . . I wanted to see you.
Why?

. . .
That night in Paris . . .
It meant something to me.

I didn't see it as a casual thing.

. . .

Did you think it was just a casual hookup for me?
. . . yes
Was it just a casual hookup for you?
no
t it was a pretty upid thing to do. or both of us.
SLAM
Ha! Yes, it was. If we'd been caught, we'd both have been fired.

Which is why, if we did it again, we should probably find a more sensible setting. Like one of our places. Ideally with drinks or dinner beforehand.

I'm asking you out, Youssef.

Y-yes,
I know you're
asking me out!!
You just
look a bit
confused
about it.
. . . sorry. I . . .
I'm new
to this.
You've never
dated? That's
okay –
No, it's just –

Only . . .
only women.
So
no
one
. . .
I actually
. . .
liked.
Sorry
I don't want to
. . . say the wrong
thing and . . .
mess
this
up
TOUCH

I don't want to rush anything, Youssef.
I just want to get to know you better.
So would you consider going on a date with me?

I'll
consider
Good. Well, then.
You have my number.

The End . . . ?

HI, MY NAME IS
HARRY
PROFILE PAGE
NAME
HARRY GREENE
BIRTHDAY
APRIL 17TH
SCHOOL YEAR (IN VOLUME ONE)
YEAR 11
PRONOUNS
HE/HIM
LIKES
• banter
• video games
• parties
DISLIKES
• studying
• uncool people
• alone time
Harry is a classic bully modeled after many boys I encountered in my school days. He's the sort of boy who sits at the back of the bus and throws food at people just to get a laugh out of his mates. This sort of boy terrified me when I was at school!

ENERGY
gum
CRISPS
BBQ
flavour
Big For Your Boots - Stormzy
0:00

Hey, my name is
Ben
PROFILE PAGE
NAME
Ben Hope
BIRTHDAY
December 1st
SCHOOL YEAR (IN VOLUME ONE)
Year 11
PRONOUNS
he/him
LIKES
• his girlfriend
• his mates
• winning
DISLIKES
• Nick Nelson
• nosy people
• rumors
Like Nick, Ben is struggling with his sexuality, but ultimately Ben deals with this by turning to destructive and abusive behaviors. I certainly like to imagine that Ben could become a better person, but Charlie doesn't need to witness that, or forgive Ben, or redeem him.

Nicotine - Panic! At The Disco
0:00

BOOF! My name is
Nellie

PROFILE PAGE

NAME
Nellie Nelson

I AM A...
Border collie

PRONOUNS
she/her

BORK! My name is

Henry

PROFILE PAGE

NAME

Henry Nelson

I AM A...

Pug

PRONOUNS

he/him

Many people don't know that Aled was first created as one of the main characters of my YA novel *Radio Silence*. He's a bit older in that book and he's the creator of an internet-famous fiction podcast called *Universe City*.

Radio People - Zapp
0:00

HALLOWEEN

Many years ago, on my art blog, I started the annual tradition of "Halloween art". Every year, I would take requests from my followers for Halloween-themed art suggestions and try to draw as many as I could during October! While there are lots that I couldn't include here due to copyright (e.g. the iconic drawing of Nick and Charlie dressed up as Sully and Mike from *Monsters, Inc.*), I've drawn several new ones especially for this book. So, if you've always wanted to see the characters of Heartstopper dressed up in Halloween costumes, or engaging in spooky activities like demon hunting, or maybe even thought about them in a horror alternate universe, this is the section for you ...

YES
OUIJA
NO
GOOD BYE

• REC
TAO: We're spending the night in the Haunted Woods of Truham, hoping to find the demon that is said to appear here and murder innocent teenagers.

• REC
DARCY: HELLO DEMON, COME AND SAY HI
ELLE: DARCY NO!
TARA: DARCY!

I- Is anyone there?
GASP

HAPPY HALLO

(Charlie saw someone in a werewolf mask)
sob
Hey, it's okay! It wasn't real!
Oh dear...

Happy Halloween!
BOO!

BOO

THE WORLD OF

Heartstopper takes place in the real world. Well, sort of, anyway. All the locations in Heartstopper could exist in the real world and some of them are even inspired by real places in our world. And while they're all quite ordinary places – bedrooms, school, the beach – they all hold special memories for Nick, Charlie, and the Heartstopper gang.

It'd be impossible for me to draw every single Heartstopper location in six pages, but here are some of the most important places in the story, and a few bits of behind-the-scenes info about them.

THE BEACH

There are three separate scenes that take place at the beach in Heartstopper so far, and two of those are at a beach I based on Herne Bay in Kent. The main difference, though, is that I made it a sandy beach in my drawings, while the real Herne Bay is a rocky beach and not the comfiest place to go sunbathing!

FORM ROOM

The form room is the most iconic location at Nick and Charlie's school. It's where they first meet! And it's where they see each other every morning and afternoon in their form group (the class where attendance is recorded and notices are read out). I wanted there to be a big window next to their seats so they're always bathed in light when they're together in the form room.

SCHOOL FIELD

Another iconic Truham location is the school field, which is home to the rugby pitch and the running track. While Charlie isn't the biggest fan of sports, Nick and Charlie have lots of happy memories of playing rugby together.

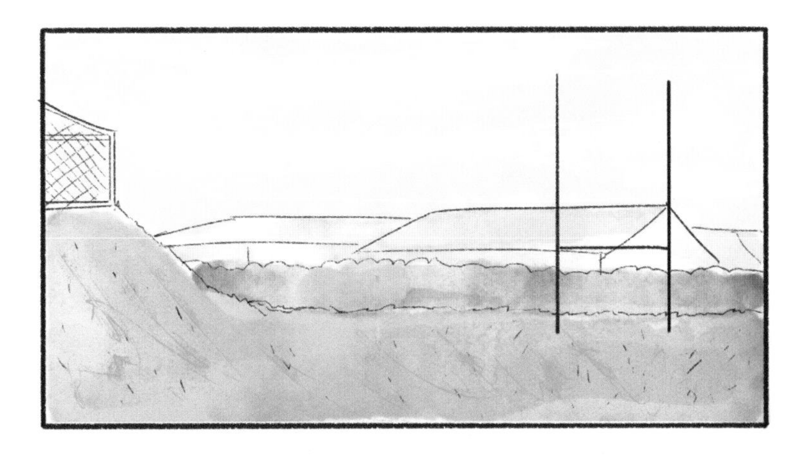

CHARLIE'S HOUSE

KITCHEN

Charlie's kitchen is a big open space that leads out on to the garden. When Nick comes over, Nick and Charlie sometimes like to sit and chat in the kitchen with cups of tea and snacks, but usually they'll just head up to Charlie's bedroom for some privacy!

LIVING ROOM

Charlie's living room – the setting of the iconic almost-hand-holding scene from Volume One – is a modern space that focuses on the big sofa, a fluffy rug, and the TV. Because the Springs are quite a big family, I imagine Charlie doesn't spend loads of his time here. He prefers to chill out in his bedroom!

CHARLIE'S ROOM

View A

View B

NICK'S HOUSE

KITCHEN

Nick's big coming-out scene takes place in the kitchen, so I wanted it to feel cozy and comforting ... which is probably why I ended up basing it on the kitchen layout of my childhood home!

LIVING ROOM

We don't see much of Nick's living room, but it's home to many a Mario Kart tournament between Nick and Charlie, as well as being the favorite hangout spot of Nick's dogs, Nellie and Henry.

NICK'S ROOM

View A

View B

MoMENTs
a heartstopper mini-comic

This mini-comic was created in 2017 and takes place during Chapter 2, just after the scene where Nick searches "am I gay" online!

AFTER THE EASTER HOLIDAYS . . .

We hung out almost every day over the Easter holidays and we kept having these . . .
moments . . .
Like when we went to the arcade and went in the photo booth . . .
Are you sure we'll both fit in there? We're tall . . .
Come on, it'll be funny!

We're definitely not gonna fit in here
We'll be fine!
Just - just sit on my leg-
No no no I'm heavy!!
Okay . . . this is cozy

FLASH
And then on another day
Nick came over to help me and my brother make my sister's birthday cake . . .

Not too much!

BLOW

You little . . .
GRAB
No no
No –
AH!
You can't win everything by just picking me up!!
I can though
?

And then there was this one evening we took his dog for a walk . . .
Th-the sky's s-so p-pretty

?

Aren't you cold?
No, not really!

Oh . . .

Um . . . there's a bug in your hair
WE NEARLY KISSED
Or like I don't know I guess he might have been trying to get a bug out of my hair but I don't know the sunset was so romantic I was CONFUSED
I like him so much
Do you think anything's gonna happen?

The end x

Hi, my name is
TORI
PROFILE PAGE
NAME
Tori Spring
BIRTHDAY
April 5th
SCHOOL YEAR (IN VOLUME ONE)
Year 11
PRONOUNS
she / her
LIKES
• alone time
• laptop
• diet lemonade
DISLIKES
• most people
• gossip
• fakeness
Tori is the first-born child of the Osemanverse. She is the first character I created for my first book, Solitaire, and she's the narrator of that book. She's always fun to write because she's so pessimistic and deadpan!

Everything in Its Right Place - Radiohead
0:00

Hello, my name is
Sahar
PROFILE PAGE
NAME
Sahar Zahid
BIRTHDAY
December 22nd
SCHOOL YEAR (IN VOLUME ONE)
Year 11
PRONOUNS
she/her
LIKES
• dark academia
• history
• guitar
DISLIKES
• people who boast
• loud parties
• PDA
Sahar loves escaping into fictional worlds and dreams of leaving the small town of Truham and going on adventures. Her favorite thing to do at school is band practice!

hand cream
THE SECRET HISTORY
DONNA TARTT
Something Has to Change - The Japanese House
0:00

Hello, my name is
Mr. Farouk
PROFILE PAGE
NAME
Youssef Farouk
BIRTHDAY
March 13th
OCCUPATION
Science teacher
PRONOUNS
he / him
LIKES
• hiking
• documentaries
• museums
DISLIKES
• social media
• spiders
• celebrities
I created Mr. Farouk and Mr. Ajayi together – I wanted to create a grumpy teacher and a sunshine teacher. Mr. Farouk is the grumpy one! He gets stressed easily, finds children quite annoying, and probably shouldn't have become a teacher.

Buses Splash with Rain - Frankie Cosmos
0:00

Hi, my name is
Mr. Ajayi
PROFILE PAGE
NAME
Nathan Ajayi
BIRTHDAY
August 28th
OCCUPATION
Art teacher
PRONOUNS
he / him
LIKES
• cocktails
• watercolor
• museums
DISLIKES
• cooking
• wearing a tie
• deep water
I created Mr. Farouk and Mr. Ajayi together – I wanted to create a grumpy teacher and a sunshine teacher. Mr. Ajayi is the sunshine one! He's super creative, has a positive outlook on life, and probably spent loads of time in the art room when he was at school.

I need my coffee
Telephone - Waterparks
0:00

WINTER

Winter is my favorite season, so every year, when December rolls around, I love to draw winter-themed Heartstopper art. Whether it's characters snuggled away from the cold, playing in the snow, or celebrating Christmas, winter Heartstopper art always puts a smile on my face!

nicholaszzzzz
435 likes
nicholaszzzzz nellie's first christmas (I think I was seven here??)
cfspring best friends
its_elles_universe oh my god
326 likes
nicholaszzzzz when ur bf comes round to watch xmas movies but just falls asleep immediately 😑

AAAAAAAAA

THE SPRINGS

Charlie, Tori, and Oliver live with their mum and dad and (sadly) no pets. While Charlie doesn't have an amazing relationship with his mum, he has a generally calm family life, and because they're mostly a family of introverts, everyone likes to do their own thing. The only exception is Oliver, who loves hanging out with his older siblings, especially when Mario Kart is involved.

Charlie's paternal grandfather is Spanish and his grandparents on his dad's side live in Almería, which is in the South of Spain. Charlie's dad spent much of his youth living in Spain! But Emilio's story of why they have a British surname changes every time he explains it...
Charlie's mum doesn't have a great relationship with her parents, so the Spring siblings don't see their maternal grandparents very often.
Emilio
Kathleen
Richard
Nancy
Omar
Sofia
Wendy
Jules
Antonio
Clara
Esther
Rosanna
Julio Spring
Jane Spring
Charlie's three paternal first cousins appear in my novella, This Winter!
Tori Spring
Charlie Spring
Oliver Spring
Oliver is eight years younger than Charlie!

THE NELSONS

Nick lives with his mum and two dogs, Nellie and Henry. His older brother, David, has moved out to go to university, but (unfortunately) still comes home for the holidays and the occasional weekend. Nick's parents divorced when he was five, so he doesn't have many memories from when his parents were still together, but he has a very close relationship with his mum, Sarah, who he can speak to about almost anything.

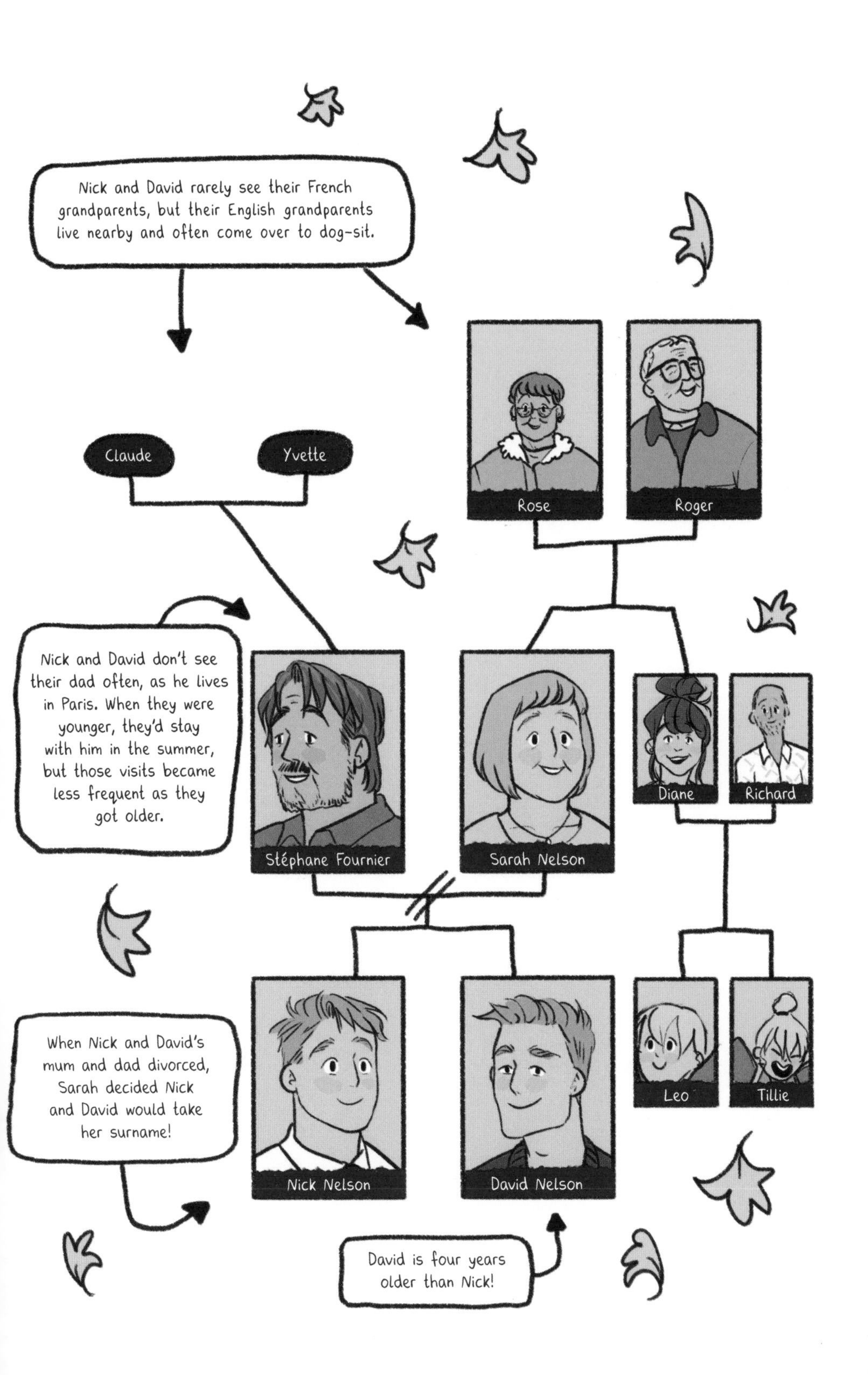
Nick and David rarely see their French grandparents, but their English grandparents live nearby and often come over to dog-sit.
Claude
Yvette
Rose
Roger
Nick and David don't see their dad often, as he lives in Paris. When they were younger, they'd stay with him in the summer, but those visits became less frequent as they got older.
Stéphane Fournier
Sarah Nelson
Diane
Richard
When Nick and David's mum and dad divorced, Sarah decided Nick and David would take her surname!
Nick Nelson
David Nelson
Leo
Tillie
David is four years older than Nick!

HOW TO DRAW

Have you ever wondered how I draw the Heartstopper characters? Perhaps you've always fancied drawing them yourself! Well, I'm here to take you through a step-by-step guide of how I draw Nick, Charlie, and Elle. Whether you're drawing with pens and pencils or on a computer or tablet, this guide will help you recreate the Heartstopper art style, and hopefully inspire you to find your own style ...

CHARLIE

1. Start with a light color or pencil – something you can erase easily. Face shapes are a circle plus a chin, so roughly sketch out the face shape.

2. The second step is to do a more detailed sketch. You can do this in a slightly darker color or heavier pencil, but still make sure you're using something you can erase. As we're drawing Charlie, you'll want to give him a pointy chin, wild and wavy hair, thick eyebrows, and pale eyes. And don't forget the signature dimples!

3. Now that you've got your sketch, it's time to line. If you're drawing traditionally, find a pen, or if you're drawing digitally, pick a pen tool and create a new layer. Now go over your sketch in more detail! And when you're done, you can erase the sketch by rubbing it out (traditional) or removing the layer (digital).

4. The final step is to add the colors! Use whatever tools you want – pens, pencils, paints, pastels ... there are so many options, whether you're working traditionally or digitally!

ALICE PRO TIP: Adding some escaping hair strands when coloring will give the hair a bit of dynamism and personality! I think hair says a lot about a person.

HEARTSTOPPER

NICK

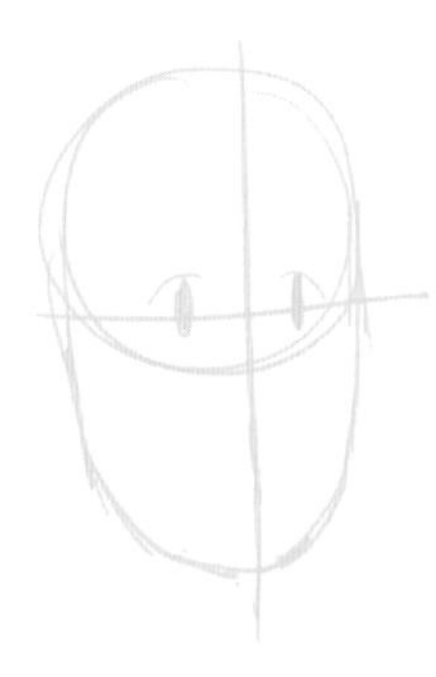

1. Start with the same step as Charlie – a rough face shape. Nick has a rounder, longer face, so keep that in mind!

2. Now add some detail to your sketch. The important things to remember for Nick are his big dark eyes, straight nose, and the iconic hair flop!

3. When lining your sketch, don't be afraid to make changes. Sometimes things that look right in the sketch end up not looking quite right when you're lining it. Obviously if you're drawing traditionally, you can't erase pen, but if you're drawing digitally, you have the power to make any changes you want!

4. And lastly, it's time to color! If you've already had a go at drawing Charlie, why not try coloring using a different tool this time? My favorites when drawing digitally are flat colors (like I've used here) or watercolors.

ALICE PRO TIP: Expressions are very reliant on eyebrow positioning! Try different eyebrow shapes and see what the effect is.

Drawing a full figure is harder than just drawing a face, for obvious reasons!

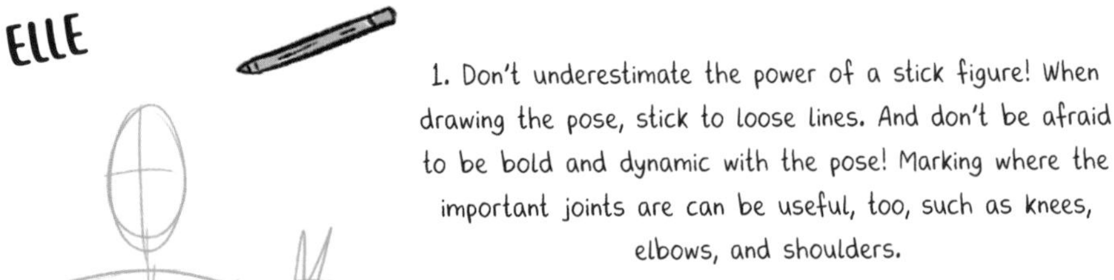

ELLE

1. Don't underestimate the power of a stick figure! When drawing the pose, stick to loose lines. And don't be afraid to be bold and dynamic with the pose! Marking where the important joints are can be useful, too, such as knees, elbows, and shoulders.

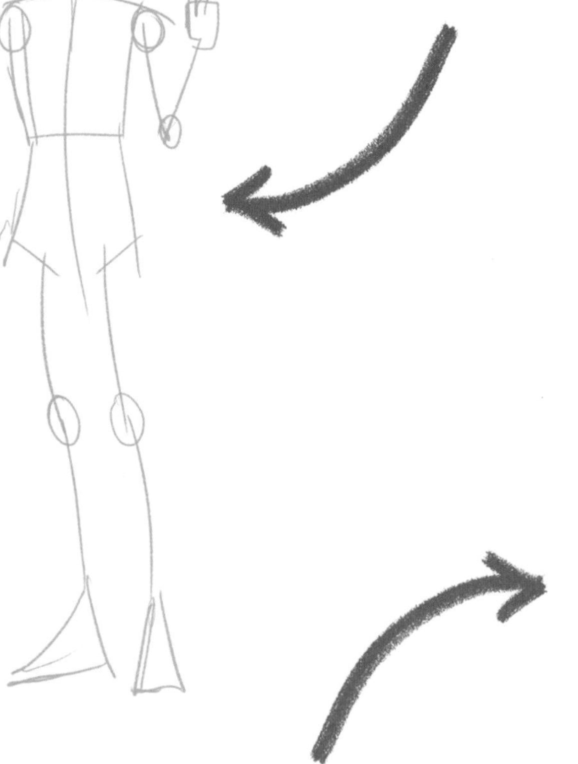

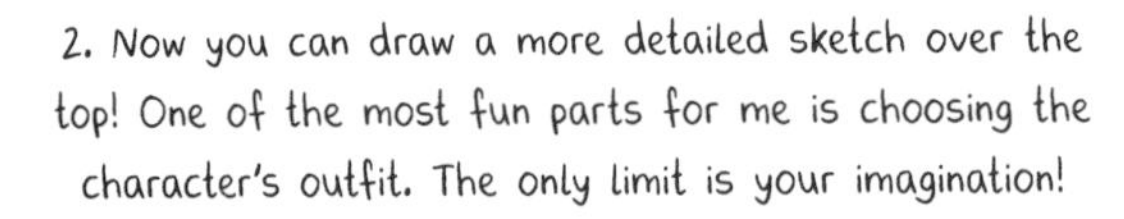

2. Now you can draw a more detailed sketch over the top! One of the most fun parts for me is choosing the character's outfit. The only limit is your imagination!

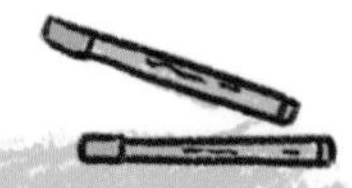

ALICE PRO TIP: Hands are notoriously difficult to draw! If you're struggling and you're not in the mood to practice, you could always draw your character with their hands in their pockets. I've done this many times when I'm not in the mood to draw hands!

It can take a lot of practice to get the hang of body proportions, gestures, and poses, but every drawing will help you improve.

3. Like when we drew Nick and Charlie, you can now start lining the sketch! Focus on loose, curved lines, and if you're stuck for how to draw something, you could always try looking at photos of people, or even a mirror, for reference.

4. Finally, it's time to color! In my examples, I've also done a little bit of shading using the "multiply" tool, which adds a bit of darker color over the top of the flat colors. It's pretty easy to do that traditionally, too – just add some more color over the top of an initial layer of color, and it adds depth to your drawing.

ALICE PRO TIP: Adding a little blush on the cheeks can bring the drawing to life! It only needs to be a slightly redder shade than the skin tone.

girlfriends ♥

Phones away, everyone! Onto the barre, please!

Let's start with pliés!

Jonesy!
Jonesy!
Jonesy
Tara! Stay focused please!
Oh- sorry, miss

TRUHAM
COMMUNITY
HALL
Hi Tara, I was just wondering if you wanted to be my girlfriend?
Tara, I really want us to be girifriends. Do you also want to be girlfriends?
?
?

Bye Tara!
See you next week!
Hi
Hi

Uh... I wasn't sure if you still wanted to meet up today because you didn't reply to my texts
Oh... Yeah, um, sorry about that
...
GRAB
?
PULL

I should have just texted you back but I started overthinking and stressing out 'cause like- I know I'm not as confident as you about being... you know... a lesbian... and I don't think I can come out yet or anything but I really like hanging out with you and kissing you so... I think... I think I really want to be your girlfriend.

I think I'm in shock right now
Why?
Because you're so pretty and cool and you wanna be my girlfriend?!
So is that a yes?
OBVIOUSLY

Are you still coming over this afternoon?
Caaaan we kiss more?
That can be arranged
Then YES
But we also have to watch Yuri on Ice. It's gay, you'll like it.
If it's gay then I'm in.
the end.

ALTERNATE
Throughout the many years I've been drawing Heartstopper art, I've always had a special place in my heart for AUs, aka "Alternate Universes." The concept is simple: you draw your characters in a different universe, which could be a different time period, or a fantasy/science-fiction world, or simply a different story scenario. It's so much fun to imagine the characters of Heartstopper meeting and interacting in other universes, and how different the story would be!
Um- now might be a good time to tell you I'm an angel
W-What!?

UNIVERSES

COUGH
COUGH

You should go without me
I'm not gonna leave you

One of my favorite AUs is "Regency Era," probably because I'm a big fan of Pride and Prejudice! I can totally imagine Nick and Charlie crushing on each other from afar in a fancy ballroom, or sneaking off to kiss in secret...
!
KISS
KISS

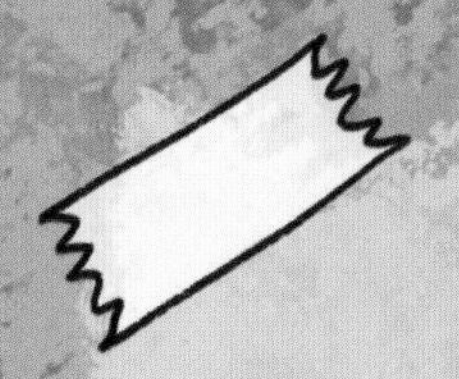

Author's Note

This book would never have existed if it were not for the support of the Heartstopper readers – online, on Tapas, Tumblr, WEBTOON, and Patreon, and in real life, buying the books all around the world. Thank you so, so much for allowing Heartstopper to shine and supporting me every step of the way.

I am also deeply grateful to all those involved in publishing Heartstopper! My agent, Claire Wilson, my editor, Rachel Wade, and everyone working on Heartstopper at Hachette and Heartstopper's international publishers.

Heartstopper has been on a wild journey, and I'm so happy to be able to work on this story. I can't wait to see what the future holds for Heartstopper!